Other Titles Available:

  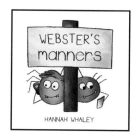

For Layla and Iris

Published by Born Digital Books.

www.borndigitalbooks.co.uk

First printing: June 2015.
Rudiment Font © Kevin Richey

ISBN-13: 978-0-9930012-4-6

Webster's Friend

Written and Illustrated
by Hannah Whaley

Webster liked to play pretend.
He dressed up all the time.

First he would
be a pirate,

then a robot
fighting crime.

So when he made a friend online, he thought he'd play a game. He had no idea that this new friend was going to do the same!

First, Webster said his name was Max
(although this was not true).

"I'm Bruno," his new friend replied.
"Nice to meet you too!"

Webster wanted to seem older.
"I'm a teenager," he said. "I never tidy up my room – I just watch TV instead."

"Me too!" typed Bruno right away.
"And I'm really tall. It means I'm good at lots
of sports, especially basketball."

"Well, I'm a champion gardener!" Webster wrote to his surprise - because he'd never planted anything, or ever won a prize.

"That's impressive," Bruno said.
"Although not to me of course,
because I know how to fly a plane..."

"And I own a horse."

"Wow!" thought Webster. "What a guy!
I don't want this to end.

I had better make up some more things
- so that he stays my friend."

But his stories got more silly, as he typed a little faster - never knowing all these fibs would end up in disaster.

"I played tennis with a dragonfly."

"I climbed the highest tree."

"One time I built a space ship and landed on the moon...

I made friends with an alien!

We are having lunch at noon."

Bruno got excited:
"I will come round right away! I would love to meet an alien – I'll find out where you stay."

"Oh no!" thought Webster. "Now I'm caught.
This is really bad.
I had better go and get some help.
I had better tell my Dad."

But on his way he passed his brother, who was ever so delighted. "I'm meeting an alien," he boasted. "And YOU are not invited!"

"I met them on the internet -
I pretended I was cool.
Now I get to hang out with them
while you have to go to school."

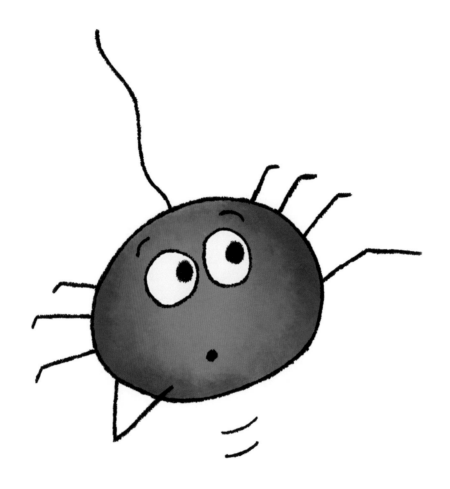

Webster was shocked! "That can't be right –
Did you say your name was Bruno?"

"Well, yes," said Jake. "I did, but
However did YOU know? "

"Because I was Max! That was me! I told fibs!"
poor Webster cried.

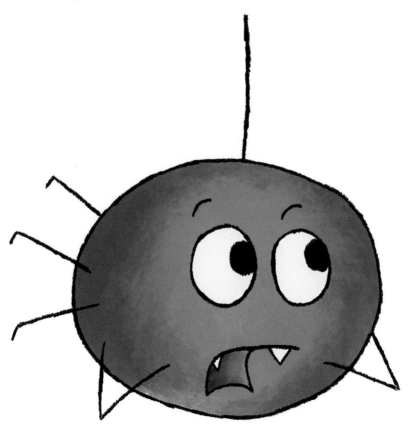

"I wanted to impress my friend
so that was why I lied."

"Oh," said Jake. "I feel so silly.
I believed it was all true."

"Me too," said Webster sheepishly.
"I didn't have a clue. I forgot that everybody
else could be pretending too."

"Let's just go back to being us –
we are best as me and you."

27514468R00018

Printed in Great Britain
by Amazon